Our Little Finnish Cousin

Clara Vostrovsky Winlow

Copyright © 2023 Culturea Editions
Text and cover : © public domain
Edition : Culturea (Hérault, 34)
Contact : infos@culturea.fr
Print in Germany by Books on Demand
Design and layout : Derek Murphy
Layout : Reedsy (https://reedsy.com/)
ISBN : 9791041826094
Légal deposit : July 2023
All rights reserved

Our Little Finnish Cousin

CHAPTER I

A FARM HOME

IT was early autumn in the Finland forest by the lake. Gold glistened from the underbrush, from the great beds of bracken, from the shining birches, from the paler aspens, and even from the prized rowans and juniper trees.

On one side where the forest grew thinner, there was a glimpse of marshy land where big whortleberries grew in profusion. Around this marshy spot a tiny path led to a succession of fields in some of which were grazing cattle, in some, queer tall haystacks, and in two smaller ones, grain still uncut.

Two children—a boy and a girl—made their way from the forest toward the lake, their hands tightly clasping birchen baskets filled with berries that they had succeeded in gathering. Reaching the shore, they silently took their places in a small boat moored under a clump of trees. Each seized an oar, and began to row with experienced measured strokes to the other side.

Both unsmiling faces had the same candid capable air, but that was the only resemblance. Ten-year-old Juhani was like his father who belonged to the Tavastian type of Finn. He was pale, with high cheek bones, thin hair, and a strong chin that seemed to say: "I won't give in! I won't give in!" He might have been taken for sulky until you met the look of sincere inquiry under his well-formed brows.

Six-year Maja was fairer. She was brown-eyed and brown-haired, like her Karelian mother who belonged to the other decided type of Finn. Despite the silent gentleness of her face, she looked as if, on occasion, she could be high spirited and even gay.

A little crowd was gathered at the landing stage to which they crossed, and more persons came hurrying up as a blast was heard from a steamer still some distance away on the lake. There were other children like themselves with baskets of birch, and women with cakes and cookies and farm produce for sale. Some of these were busily knitting while they waited to offer their wares. Most prominent among all thus gathered was a rather short, sturdy girl, who seemed entirely indifferent to the fact that the kerchief tied around her head was not at all becoming. This was Hilja, who, although only eighteen, already held the important position of pier-master.

At last, amid much commotion, the steamer came up. The passengers stepped ashore and bought many of the good things offered. But even when all were sold there was no sign of the steamer's departure. The big stacks of wood piled on the wharf, that were to serve the steamer for fuel, had first to be carried aboard. For this there was help in plenty. Men, women, and children were eager to have their services accepted. A couple of foreigners grew restless at the delay, but no one else betrayed any impatience, having been brought up, no doubt, on the Finnish proverb, "God did not create hurry."

The pier-master shouted something when it was all in, and the steamer, with many toots, departed. The people scattered until only Juhani and Maja remained to watch a heavily laden timber barge go slowly by on its way to the coast. Before it passed Juhani had nudged Maja to show her the pennies he had earned by carrying wood. With the slightest possible twinkle of mischief, Maja at first kept her own fist tightly closed. "Oh, show what you have!" Juhani exclaimed somewhat contemptuously, at which Maja opened her hand and showed twice as many pennies that her sweet face, as well as the nice berries, had brought her.

Juhani showed his surprise by staring and staring until Maja closed her hand again, explaining half in apology, "It was from the foreigners," and led the way to their boat.

Again they rowed silently over, anchored their boat in a little cove, and then walked rapidly across the fields. Maja began to hum a folk song, to which Juhani soon whistled a tune while he kept one hand on a sheathed knife, called a pukko, hanging from the belt around his waist. It was no wonder he was conscious and proud that it hung there. When his father had given it to him a few days before, he had said, "You are beginning to do man's work, Juhani, and so I think that you deserve a man's knife." Nor was it a cheap knife. Its leather sheath was tipped with brass and very prettily ornamented with a colored pattern.

Both children were barefoot and both walked with equal unconcern over stubble and sharp stones. At the edge of the last field Maja glanced inquiringly at her brother and then broke into a run. Juhani did not follow her example at first, but, when he did, he easily overtook her near a square farmhouse painted a bright red, but with doors and windows outlined in white. Against this house, reaching from the ground to the black painted roof, was a ladder to be used in case of fire. Up this Juhani ran, waving his hand to his sister when at the top.

Near this house were three storehouses, one for food, one for clothes and one for implements. Further away were cow houses, and a stable, the loft of which was used for storing food in winter, and as a bedroom for the maid servants in summer. There was also a small pig sty built of granite, a stone of which Finland has so much that it has been said it would be possible to rebuild all of London with it and still leave the supply apparently undiminished. Neat, strong fences of slanting wood enclosed these buildings.

Off by itself was an outbuilding more important in a way than any of these, the bath-house, which in Finland is never missing.

An older girl of about fourteen with a blue kerchief on her head was drawing water from a well near the kitchen door. As she emptied the bucket made of a pine trunk and attached to a long pole weighted at the end, she called to Juhani, who had just jumped from the ladder: "Hurry! The pastor has come to stay till we go to church to-morrow and he wants to ask you some Bible questions."

Without waiting for her, Juhani followed Maja, who had already entered the kitchen bright with shining copper, stopping first, however, to wipe his feet on a mat made of pine branches laid one above another.

This kitchen led directly into a pleasant living-room, with a tall china tiled stove, some chairs, a big sofa, a table, and a carved cupboard. Here were several odd beds too, that did not look like beds at all. They were beds shut up for the day. At night they would be pulled open. A small loom stood in one corner. Strips of home-made carpet were laid on the yellow painted floor.

On one wall hung a picture which had lately had a peculiar fascination for Maja. It represented Katrine Mansdottir, a beautiful peasant woman with a sad romantic history. She lived when Finland was under Swedish rule. King Eric the Fourteenth had been captivated by her winsomeness when he first saw her selling fruit on the street. He had her taken to his castle and educated her like a princess. When she was old enough he married her, much to the dissatisfaction of his conservative courtiers. Later the King was deposed and cast into prison. Here his wife showed her gratitude for all that he had done for her, sharing his imprisonment and ministering to him until his death. Then she renounced her crown and retired to live among the loyal Finns who loved her for the friendship that she had always shown them.

On the most comfortable chair in the room sat the pastor, a man who looked so serious that one wondered if he ever smiled. No one who knew his duties and responsibilities could wonder at this. Among them were visiting the widely scattered members of his parish, comforting them in sorrow and distress, helping them with advice when needed. Just outside the nearest village, on the other side of the lake, he had a little patch of land of his own which he cultivated when he could, to help out his slender salary.

The children greeted the pastor like an old friend, and seating themselves sedately on chairs opposite him stiffened up in anticipation of the questions that he would ask them.

Around four o'clock everything in the room became evening colored, and the mother came in and invited all into the kitchen for dinner. There was an abundance of simple food, — salt fish, meat and potatoes, hard rye bread, mead and coffee, of which latter even little Maja drank her share.

The first part of the meal made one think of a Quaker meeting, it was so very quiet; but after the mead had been passed around and the coffee poured, a sparkle came to the eyes of all, and even the pastor's face took on a genial glow as, prompted by kind inquiries, he related some of his recent experiences.

"You know poor old Yrjo (George)," he said, "who is now one of my people. Well, he's trying to learn to read and write and having a hard time doing it. You see, he never had a chance earlier in life, for he used to live way up north on the outskirts of Lapland. He is doing all this because—well, I guess you can guess why—. Yes, he wants to be married, and you know how strict our law is that no pastor shall marry men or women unless they know how to read and write. I think he'll learn, for he's dogged. He's already built himself a shack on my grounds not to waste time in coming and going. When I told him this morning that he was making progress he was as delighted as a child."

Then he told of a recent visit to a big dairy farm, of the long low buildings with ice chambers here and there. "It was a great pleasure," he said, "to see how neatly everything is kept. All the floors and walls are of blue and white tile, and the windows of stained glass—a pretty sight. I can't forget the rows of shelves with their big earthenware vessels of rich-looking milk and cream. In one room women dressed in white were putting up butter for export. I agree with those who think that dairying is going to grow in importance here. It certainly seems to pay our farmers better than farming."

"I am going to be a dairy man," said Juhani.

"And I am going to a University and be an architect," piped in little Maja quite as decidedly.

At this the family laughed, but the pastor remarked seriously, "It's well to make plans early. There are many women who are succeeding in architecture, little Maja."

"Yes," remarked the mother, "and Maja has an aunt in Helsingfors who is among the number."

As it was Saturday night the usual preparations had been made for a family bath, and the kindly pastor who was not considered an outsider was invited to share in it as a matter of course. Every one seemed to look to this bath as a great pleasure. After the pastor had accepted, Juhani, with face glowing, ran at once to show the bath whisks that he had himself made.

"I made a lot of them in the summer," he explained, "for then the leaves are soft."

"Go take them to the bath house and steep them in hot water," said his father, "and see that the maids have not forgotten to strew fresh straw on the floor."

"May I not get ready first," asked Juhani. And when his father nodded, he slipped off his clothes and ran naked to where the bath house stood alone not far from the lake.

The little structure was made of pine logs on a foundation of moss and stones. The roof was thatched. Over the door the farmer had carved the Finnish proverb: "The Church and the Sauna (Bath-house) are holy places." Within, on one side, was a stone oven, while opposite this was a series of wooden steps to the ceiling. These were covered with straw.

When Juhani entered, an old woman servant was already there poking at the big fire. Now and then she threw on water so that it was quite steamy when the other members of the family came trooping in. Juhani at once seized Maja around the waist, all his shyness evidently left outside, and twirled her around until she shouted for him to stop.

It grew hotter and hotter in the room and more and more steamy as the different members climbed on the step-like platforms and beat themselves with the birch twigs which now gave forth a pleasant fragrance.

Juhani and Maja had also mounted the steps, but every once in a while they would jump down and try to whip each other on the back and legs.

When all had perspired enough, they took turns in sitting on a chair and letting the old woman give each a quick massage and a wash down with cold water. Then oh, what a race there was for the lake, into which all plunged with shouts of laughter! Then out again and a race for home. Maja somehow got a big start and came in a foot ahead of her brother who, when he saw what she was after, almost tumbled over her in his eagerness to win.

CHAPTER II

SUNDAY

PREPARATIONS for going to church next morning were soon made. Some things that we should consider unusual were taken, including a big lunch and a couple of hammocks. Two row boats carried the party some distance down the lake to a much larger boat, called the Church Boat. It was already half filled. After a short wait, other peasants arrived, greeted their friends soberly and sat down.

The men had on somber-looking suits, with big felt hats and high boots. The women's costumes varied, although the majority had on black shapeless jackets with a white kerchief crossed under the chin; some, however, had on bright bodices, embroidered aprons, and blue or crimson kerchiefs. Most of the women carried their prayer-books wrapped in white handkerchiefs. When all were seated, the young women, as well as the young men, seized hold of the oars and the boat left the pier.

It was a slow journey, stops being made at a few places where people stood waiting. It was rather solemn, too; there was no idle chatter; at the minister's suggestion, however, hymns were sung.

The Lutheran Church, at which the party at last arrived, was a plain building both inside and out. It was built entirely of timber and had a separate bell tower. As the people walked in, the women all took their places on one side, the men on the other.

The services lasted until three in the afternoon. Maja yawned and almost put herself asleep counting the stitches in the woman's jacket in front of her. But when it was all over and the people filed out of the building, they seemed to leave some of their somberness there. They gathered in groups and together departed either for a swim in the lake or with hammocks and lunches for a picnic in the silent woods.

Things tasted so good out of doors that Maja and Juhani smiled much at each other, although Juhani would always put on a particularly serious look afterwards. Then the two swung on one of the hammocks and also on a huge swing near the Church. "Come on for a ramble with us in the woods," two passing children of their own age called to them. "Come," said Maja, taking hold of Juhani's hand, and away they went over the greenish gray mosses through the rosy and pale yellow underbrush. There were bright red cranberries here and there with which they filled their pockets as they discussed, not church affairs, but wood nymphs, the kind ugly tomtar or brownies, and the little gray man in the woods who has a fiery tail.

Suddenly Maja stopped, looking so scared that all followed her example. "What is it?" asked her brother.

"A brownie!" Maja could hardly make herself heard.

The boys laughed at her as they rushed forward and made a big brown squirrel scamper away into the branches of a tree.

"Nevertheless I'd like to believe that there were brownies around," Juhani confessed when the girls had come up. "Do you know that they are so kind that on Christmas they bring a gift to every animal that lives near?"

The others nodded. "I'd rather see one than a wood nymph," one of them declared. "I'd be afraid of her. My! but she must be ugly from behind if she's really hollow there as they say. She's apt to do you harm too, if you see her from the back."

By this time they had reached a little one-room hut evidently deserted, for the door swung on only one hinge. Before they peeked in, Juhani, with a curious look on his face, cautioned each to say "Good Day to all here" on entering even if they saw no one, for a Tomty might be hidden in some corner.

It was a very old type of house. The upper half of the walls were stained black. There was a big fire place but no chimney, the smoke having evidently been allowed to escape through a hole in the roof.

A long thin piece of resinous wood was still fastened to one wall. This was called a pare, and when lit served instead of lamp or candle.

There was a small clearing around the house, and half buried in leaves near the door was an old-time harrow that had once been formed from a bundle of stout fir top branches.

Later they paused to ask for a drink of water at a small two-room cottage of unhewn, unpainted wood surrounded by a little pasture but with no garden or other sign of cultivation around, nothing but the vast impressive forest. A savage-looking dog that looked as if it might have been crossed with a fox, snarled at them but was called away by a very old woman who explained that she was there alone, her son having lately gone to a timber camp. "He'll come back with enough money," she added with a trembling voice, "to see us through the winter, which is going to be a hard one."

"Why do you say that, Granny?" asked Juhani.

"Couldn't you see it for yourself," the old woman returned rather sharply, "by the great number of berries?"

"Are you not lonely here?" Maja inquired with sympathy.

"Aye, lonely," repeated the woman, "but contented too, for have I not the forest with me day and night and is it not a part of my very soul?"

A long drawn whistle here made the children realize that the church parties were breaking up and that they must make haste to return, so thanking the old woman they raced back apparently as fresh as if they had not already had a long tramp. Where the forest was thickest it was quite dark. "If it gets any darker," said Maja, "we'll have to stop and pray to the Twilight Maiden to spin for us a thread of gold to lead us safely home."

"There are also others to help us," said Juhani, and half playfully he called on all the woodland fairy folk whose names are found in the great Finland epic, "The Kalevala": on Mielikki, hostess of the forest; Tuometar, nymph of the bird cherry; Katejatar, nymph of the juniper; Pillajatar, nymph of the mountain ash; Matka-Teppo, god of the road; Hongatar, ruler of the pines; Sinetar, that beauteous elf who paints the flowers the blue of the sky, and on Sotka's daughter who protects wild game from harm.

CHAPTER III

THE END OF AUTUMN

THE next day Maja had to stay in the house to help while her mother and sister baked, for they were to have a talko, that is, neighbors had been invited over to help with the last of the harvesting. "Have lots of good things to eat," Juhani called as he followed his father out to help in one of the fields. Here a number of peasants were driving long poles into the ground at regular intervals; to these they fastened eight outstretched arms, the ends of which were curved upwards. On these arms hay that had been cut with sickles was carefully arranged that it might dry.

While this was being done, the grain that had been dried some time before was being baked in an outside oven or kiln not far from the hay barn, a big long building with a corrugated roof.

This baking makes the Finnish grain in demand for seed in other countries, for it drives away the damp and kills all insects that might injure the germ.

By evening all the work was finished, and the merry group of peasant men and women who had given their help trooped, singing, to the house. A big supper awaited them and as they sat down, the men on one side of the table, the women on the other, all showed the splendid appetites which the work in the fields had given them.

As soon as the supper was over, the floor was cleared, and all joined in dancing the national dance, called the jenka, during which a warmth of feeling was displayed that belied their reputation for being stolid, and that no stranger, who might have seen the men and women on their way to church the day before, would have believed possible.

After this the weather grew less pleasant; the sky was often dull and overcast; cold raw winds began to blow and there was much fog and sleet. During this time there was a certain flurry in the farm house, for Juhani, young as he was, had gained his father's permission to accompany an uncle to a lumber camp some distance to the north.

At the first fall of snow they left. It was a long drive they had, one that grew colder after the middle of the day. The air, which was very still, had a frostiness to it that nipped Juhani's nose and face. But neither he nor his uncle grumbled. The faces of both had a peculiarly similar look of patient endurance. It was not until toward evening that they came to a rolling swampy country where a big body of woodmen were already at work at the rude shelters that were to form the camp. For one night a batch of new men had to lie around the camp fire, turning one side, then the other to the heat, for there were not enough huts yet built.

Juhani was put to work almost at once in picking up chips and doing all sorts of odds and ends, for he had only been allowed to go on condition that he was willing to make himself useful. Later he was regularly sent alone twice a week through the forest to a peasant farm for milk and eggs. The coming and going for these took all of a day. Sometimes the forest was dark and silent; at other times birds called to him, and wild animals, strangely tame, would peep out from the snow-covered brush at him.

Once a merry squirrel enticed him into an old overgrown path. He continued to follow it even after he had lost track of the squirrel until he came to two branches, one of which he decided led in the direction of his destination.

After wandering about for an hour and finding that the trees and the brush were growing denser and denser he grew somewhat alarmed and tried to retrace his steps.

He soon found that this was impossible. Here it occurred to him that if he could get to the top of a tree he might have a better idea of where he was and what to do. So dropping his pail, he scrambled up the nearest willow. This was not high enough to give much of an outlook, and, getting down again, he cast longing eyes on a tall fir with no low branches.

With difficulty he dragged a small uprooted juniper to it and placing it against the trunk, with its help he managed to reach the lowest branch. It was then an easy task to climb to the top of the tree.

There was a very fair outlook from the top but no sign of the farmhouse for which he was bound. There was one thing comforting however. It was that at some distance away something glittered like water.

With a grunt Juhani let himself down and then stood in thought. Only for a moment did he allow himself to do this. He was too well aware of the shortness of the days to dally. Drawing his pukko (knife) he began to hew his way through the thick underbrush, over the springy soil, in the direction of what he knew must be the lake.

Now and then fallen tree trunks had to be scaled. Twice his feet caught in tangled vines and threw him. Several times he had to take the time to climb trees to assure himself that he was going in the right direction. And all the time he had the consciousness that night was descending.

It was already dusk when he reached the lake where, to his great relief, he recognized the spot by means of a big bowlder as being within half a mile of camp.

He saw, however, that in a very few minutes it would be too dark to go further. The only thing to do was to wait until the moon rose. So gathering together as much of the brush as he could, he started it burning and then lay down before it to try to get a little rest.

Despite the fire, which continually had to be replenished, it was very cold and he found it necessary to turn constantly first one side, then the other towards the flames to be at all comfortable.

At last the fire went out and there was nothing left for Juhani to do except sit with his back to the trunk of a nearby tree and wait. When the moon came out, it was a very stiff boy who arose and followed stumblingly the banks of the lake to camp.

Here he found a group of men with his Uncle in the lead, getting ready to start a hunt for him. As soon as he had stammered out his story to his Uncle the latter shook him angrily by the shoulder and ordered him to bed. "Don't you ever try anything of the kind again; at least not while you are on an errand for me," he called after him. And Juhani never did.

The boy won the favor of a driver of one of the short sledges on which the cut-down trees, rough hewn with axes and with the bark peeled off, were drawn, and he sometimes had a ride with him to the lake where men stalked the logs on the banks. On these trips, although he said nothing, he hardly knew whether he admired most how the driver guided the horses over the difficult ground or the intelligence of the alert little Finnish horses themselves.

Sometimes, instead of these trips, he had an opportunity to watch the actual cutting down of the trees. He would sometimes quiver in sympathy as a tree quivered before dashing down against the other trees, perhaps remaining suspended a moment, then coming with a crash to the ground and raising a flurry of snow.

Once a tree was down it was ready to be cleared of branches and then sawed into logs.

In the evening the spring journey of the logs, when they would be floated down the lake and out to sea, was often discussed. Juhani learned how men with long hooks were stationed at the narrow or rocky places on the water to keep the logs from getting blocked. This was difficult and often dangerous. Sometimes it led to loss of life.

While on the lake, the logs would be collected and chained together to form great rafts. Several of these would be fastened behind each other and drawn by a small tug. On these rafts the men would build themselves little huts on which they would live, for it is slow work to get the logs from the forests to the mills. Indeed it almost always takes one or two summers at least.

Sometimes instead of these stories, the men would sing rough songs that sounded out there in the wilds more weird and melancholy than they really were. Sometimes they discussed the future of Finland. There was one fellow among them to whom Juhani loved to listen. He remembered long the man's reply to a particularly pessimistic statement. "Our future depends on ourselves. Have we not the sea? Does it not stand for power and freedom? Shame, I say, on those who do not see it!"

Things in camp went along quietly enough until near the end of the season, when two of the men had a fight which might have ended seriously had they not been separated in time, for both had drawn their pukkos (knives).

Before Juhani left for home the driver invited him to come on a trip much further east than they were stationed. His uncle consented. It gave Juhani an opportunity to see the very primitive and wasteful agricultural methods that are still practiced in Finland in out-of-the-way places, that of burning down the forest to fertilize the land.

They spent the first night with the owner of a place on which this was done. He did his best to entertain them well.

After they had had supper the family gathered around the big rude fireplace, and while the fire crackled and a drink of some kind was passed around the talk drifted to the future prospects of the country. Then the peasant proprietor told of the time when the deposed Tzar of Russia, Nicholas II, through the Manifesto of February fifteenth, 1899, had tried to deprive Finland of most of her independence. "I heard through my young son who had just returned from further South, that signatures for a petition to the Tzar were being sought. 'They shall not lack mine,' I told my wife. It was bitterly cold even for one used to severe months of blinding snow, but I put on my skis and made my way through the dense forest in the face of a harsh wind, to the nearest settlement Here I learned that a messenger gathering signatures had just left. Without stopping for food or drink, I followed the direction he had taken through a frozen swamp and came up with him just before nightfall. And there, with nothing to be seen but snow around us, I signed the paper and returned to the settlement while he went on for another hour to the neighboring hamlet."

"I know of a case to match that somewhat," said the driver. "After the Tzar's Manifesto, a well-to-do farmer, who lived too far away to go to Helsingfors, wrote a petition himself to the Tzar, had it signed by the family, servants and those nearest, and then forwarded it."

Here the old grandmother, an intelligent looking peasant woman, with a brown plaid shawl tightly pinned around her neck, took the lead in the conversation, harking back to older times when she had known Elias Lönnrot who made the folk songs he gathered into a whole as the great Finnish epic, the "Kalevala." This was evidently a favorite subject with her. "I was only a young girl," she said, "when he came as a physician to Kajana, which is a place of which it was then said there were two streets, 'Along one go pigs when it's wet, along the other the inhabitants when it's dry.' Lönnrot was a strong fine fellow, very gentle. People used to say he would cry if he happened to kill a fly. He was rather careless about his clothes. I met him one day just as he was starting on one of his searches for folk songs. He was dressed like a peasant, with a short pipe in his mouth and a staff in his hand. A small flute hung from his button-hole, while a valise and gun were slung on his back. After he came back we spoke of nothing for weeks except his adventures. In one place he was taken for a tramp and found it impossible to secure any sort of vehicle to take him on his way. In another village the people thought him a wizard. They wouldn't give him any food. He remembered that an eclipse of the sun would take place that day. 'I'll make the sun die,' he said, 'if you don't attend to my wants.' The people laughed and hooted, but when the sun actually did disappear they were badly frightened and begged him on their knees to make it come back and brought him all kinds of good things to eat."

"It seems to me," said her son reflectively, "that Lönnrot published something else besides the 'Kalevala.'"

"Indeed he did," said the grandmother quickly, proud of her knowledge, "why, I've taught you many a verse given in the Kanteletaar (the Daughter of the Kantele). It contains about seven hundred ancient songs and ballads."

Juhani and the driver were somewhat surprised at hearing all this at such a far off place. They would have gladly continued the conversation had it not been necessary to retire early to be prepared for the journey to the north on the morrow.

CHAPTER IV

LAPLANDERS

A HEAVY snow fell during the night. After they had had breakfast, Juhani and the driver found two pulkas (boat shaped sleighs) awaiting them. To each of these there was harnessed reindeer of a dark gray color, with huge branching antlers. There was only one rein for each of those in the pulkasto hold.

"Notice the reindeer's foot," Juhani's companion bade him. "See how broad and flexible it is. It is divided, too, and so spreads when it touches the snow."

"How can I get the reindeer to stop?" asked Juhani anxiously.

"Well, if you really need to stop and he refuses," replied the driver, "all you have to do is to fall out."

Their host wrapped furs around them as each took his place in one of the sleds hardly big enough to hold even one person. Then while his wife held the deer, the farmer showed Juhani how to wrap the rein properly around his wrist. This being managed, the wife let go, and they were off.

The country through which they now passed was tiresomely flat and covered with small birch and fir trees. After they had gone some distance it began to snow in thick cloud-like masses and the wind began to blow the snow about as if in violent play. Juhani did very well considering that this was his first reindeer ride. He managed to stay in the sled even when the reindeer bumped it hard against the trees. Fortunately the deep furrows in the road helped steady the sleighs, and Juhani began to feel proud of himself when finally the Lapp settlement came into view. Whether it was the sight of it or something else, Juhani did not know, but just then the reindeer suddenly swerved in such a way that Juhani was pitched out. He arose quickly and called to the reindeer to stop, but in vain. His companion was far ahead and so, somewhat angry and mortified, he made his way as best he could on foot the short distance still remaining.

These Lapp settlements in Northern Finland are few in number. It is said that there are not more than two thousand Lapps in Finland. The Finnish word Lapp or Lappu means Land-End folk. The Lapps use another name for themselves; it is Samelats and for their country, Same. Many of the Lapps are fishermen, but there are also forest and mountain Lapps.

One wonders how they could get along without the reindeer, which furnishes them with milk, meat, and even clothing, besides drawing their sledges. Because of these animals the Lapps prefer the open country where reindeer moss is plentiful. When it is not found, the spruce tree serves as a substitute, and a very extravagant one, for nearly a hundred trees are needed yearly for one reindeer.

When Juhani came up, he found the whole village surrounding his friend, who laughing, advanced with a muscular, well-proportioned Lapp to him. The Lapp shook his hand and assured him gravely that no one thought the worse of him for the mishap.

This Lapp was dressed in a loose reindeer costume reaching below the knees and fitting closely about the throat. It was adorned with gay trimmings of blue and scarlet and yellow. On his feet were soft, pliable skin boots.

He led them to the largest hut. Juhani noticed the quarters of frozen reindeer meat hanging from the branches of the trees near it and also the buckets full of frozen reindeer milk.

When they had entered, they seated themselves on the floor on skins and waited while snow was brought in, placed in a kettle over the fire, melted, and coffee made. This and food was soon placed before them. The latter consisted of reindeer meat, a kind of rye and barley bread, milk and a strong oily cheese. It tasted very good to Juhani after his cold walk. When he had eaten enough to satisfy himself as well as his hospitable hosts, he was shyly invited to join in an outside game with a group of dark-skinned children with straight silky brown hair, broad flat faces and noses, and very round eyes compared to their elders. These children looked like funny little bears, wrapped as they were in fur.

Two of the boys carried wooden sticks which they drove into the snow. These were made so that a stone could rest on the top. Each child tried his best to see how many of these he could knock off with snowballs in a given time.

Juhani found himself far behind his little friends. He was not so good a shot, and he lacked their quickness in making the balls. But he kept on trying.

In the afternoon when it grew too dark and cold to remain longer out of doors (it was thirty degrees below zero), two of the children went with Juhani into the unventilated hut, and sitting down near the fire took out their knives and began to carve. Juhani watched the older of the two, a boy about his own age, and soon saw that he was making a running reindeer on the handle of a knife. Great was his surprise next morning to have this presented him. The mother, in the meantime, had just laid down some reindeer intestines that she was making into gloves.

"How many reindeer have you?" Juhani asked the Lapp boy.

"Oh, nearly a thousand," the latter answered carelessly.

"What a number of uses you put them to! I wish you would tell me all of them."

The Lapp boy smiled. "To tell all would take me all day. I will tell you a few though. We make butter and cheese from their milk, eat their flesh as food, make our beds and tents, of their skins; their tendons give us our thread and many of our eating utensils are made out of their antlers."

"It must be much trouble to milk the reindeer every day," Juhani remarked.

"But we don't milk them every day," the Lapp boy quickly put in. "Only about twice a week. Oftener it would certainly be much trouble."

Juhani wanted to know still more. "Since the reindeer are loose, how can they find food when the ground is covered with snow several feet deep?" he asked.

"They can smell it," returned the Lapp. "They never make a mistake. As soon as theysmell it, they scrape at the snow with their feet and nose until they get to it."

After another meal all gathered still closer to the log fire to listen to news of the outside world. For a long time the woodman talked, and then, growing tired, he begged the Lapp mother to tell some stories.

This she did in the Finnish language, which, like all the rest of her family, she spoke well. Soon Juhani was listening to the most marvelous tales, of giants as big as mountains with one enormous eye, of ugly witches that fly about like bats at night, and of frightful goblins that do much harm. Then, changing her tone, she softly told the story of the goddess, Nyavvinna, the kindly daughter of the Sun, a being who first caught and tamed the reindeer and gave them to the Lapps for their comfort and joy.

"Will you tell our fortune?" asked the woodman driver, eying her somewhat askance, when she had stopped. She smiled good naturedly at him, and going to a rude cabinet took from it a kind of drum by means of which she foretold a pleasant return journey on the morrow.

Juhani watched her with simple curiosity; his companion, however, was plainly uneasy, and when they were alone for a minute before lying down to sleep, he whispered, "Awfully uncanny folks, these Lapps are."

The next morning, too, despite the kindly parting, it was plain to Juhani that he was glad to get away. They had another exhilarating ride behind the reindeer. It had a delightful tang to it, a trace of wildness, to which something, even in Juhani's stolid nature, responded.

When they had left their sleds at the home of their Finnish friends the driver grew talkative and told Juhani many stories of other trips to Lapland, one the summer before to this same family. He laughed when he thought of the children. "They would have had a pleasant time gathering berries," he said, "had it not been for the mosquitoes. There were so many of these that they had to wear a sort of mosquito net fastened around the waist. When they tore these or objected too much, their mother rubbed tar all over their hands and faces. My! but they did look funny then," and he laughed so heartily that Juhani could not help but join him.

The man had many other interesting things to tell, for his experiences had been varied. Among other things he explained the old system still in use in parts of Finland of getting tar, an important Finnish industry.

"Those are fine tar trees," he said, when they had come to a clump of fir and larch. "Nothing better. Do you know how they work the thing? Well, the wood, after being cut, is piled high on a big platform that slopes from all sides to the center where there is an opening into a vat underneath. This pile is covered over with a thick layer of earth and grass and then lit from below. It smolders for several days until the pile sinks and a flame springs up. When the tar begins to flow it is caught in barrels. Shafts are afterwards attached to these barrels and they are then drawn by horses to the nearest water and loaded on boats for the coast.

"These boats are built to shoot the rapids. There is no iron used in them, the fir planks being bound together with wooden fibers. They don't weigh much so that they give in to slight shocks. Wood only three-fourths of an inch thick separates one from the water. The boats are about thirty by three feet, very long and narrow, you see, yet big enough to hold about twenty barrels, with high sides to keep out the foam.

"I tell you it takes skill and nerve to steer one of these boats. The pilots have to have a license. Besides the pilot, the crew generally consists of two men or a man and a woman. I wasn't much older than you are now when I first went in one. We started at Kajana on the Ulea River. My! how the boat did skim along! It seemed as free as a bird. I held my breath most of the time. And what a shock it was when it went plunk into the rapids which extend many miles! I'll never forget that first ride and the peculiar joy I felt at the danger. The last rapids are the Pyhakoski or Sacred Rapids. They are twelve miles long, but the trip over them took us barely twenty minutes. Here you can see the slope of the stream. Every second you go faster. Now you have to avoid a whirlpool, now a rock; sometimes both. I thought I'd just go deaf from the roar of the waters. When we reached smooth water again I thought I really was deaf, the silence was so overpowering."

"What causes the rapids?" asked Juhani.

"It's the enormous bowlders," responded his companion. "The rapids are mighty pretty. I've seen our largest waterfall, too. It's in a narrow gorge at Imatra and is sixty feet high. How many lakes make it, do you think? They say it is a thousand! There are always lots of tourists gazing at it and listening to its hissing and sputtering and roaring. When you first hear it you think there is a storm brewing. The spray is tossed thirty feet into the air and looks like a mass of rainbows."

CHAPTER V

SCHOOL

SCHOOL opened later that year than usual, to last until June. There was to be a vacation of three weeks at Christmas with an occasional week in between, as well as on special days.

Two languages were studied by all the children, Finnish and Swedish instead of Finnish and Russian as might have been expected from Finland's connection with Russia. The teacher told the children that there had been a time when all schooling was Swedish, the Finnish tongue being considered too uncouth for culture. "Happily," he would always add, "that time is past. It was unjust, for eighty-six per cent of the inhabitants are Finns. We are now fully awake." All the children had manual training, the girls being taught cooking, sewing and darning, the boys woodwork and carpentry. The schoolhouse was surrounded by trees, and once a week, at least, the teacher talked of the necessity of conserving them.

The teacher lived near the school in a furnished house provided by the country people. Around it was enough grazing land for a cow. The people saw, too, that he always had a sufficient supply of firewood.

When Maja and Juhani reached the schoolhouse on the first day they found all the names by which Finland is sometimes known beautifully written on the blackboard. There were "Strawberry Land," "The Land of a Thousand Lakes," "The Land of a Thousand Heroes," "The Land of a Thousand Isles," "Marsh Land," and "Last Born Daughter of the Sea." "This last name our country has earned," the master explained, "because it is in fact still rising out of the sea. As for 'Land of a Thousand Lakes' that should rather be the 'Land of Many Thousand Lakes.' Let all these names merely serve to remind you," he concluded, "of our duty to our country and our determination not to give up that freedom to which we feel ourselves entitled."

The singing of the Finnish National Hymn followed:

"Our Land, our Finnish Fatherland!

Ring out dear name and sound!

No hill nor dale, nor sea-worn strand,

Nor lofty mountain whitely grand,

There is more precious to be found

That this—our fathers' ground."

What Juhani liked best at school that year perhaps, was his connection with the School Paper. Every Saturday night the higher grades, beginning with the one in which he now was, met at the schoolhouse to consider original contributions to it. Both poetry and prose were submitted, and also charades and plays. Juhani won some praise for an article entitled "What We Owe to the Trees." In this he spoke of the vast number of trees in Finland, but particularly of the uses to which they were put. "The birch is one of our best friends. I may not wear birch shoes but many peasants do. From its twigs we make brooms and bath whisks; from its bark, baskets and cups. Its blocks are fed to our locomotives and steamboats, and its leaves provide food for our cattle. In time of need, when crops fail, we even make bread from its bark."

Once a month came Guest Day and the children worked hard to do themselves and the teacher credit, for then the fathers, mothers and friends invited had the right to ask the pupils questions. An entertainment was always provided; sometimes there were tableaux, sometimes a play. These were always followed by refreshments.

This year, at the first of these nights, Juhani was honored by having an introductory recitation from the Finnish poet Topelius. A part of it is:

"On the world's farthest peopled strand

Fate gave to us a Fatherland,

The last where man his foot has set,

Daring the North Pole's threat;

The last and wildest stretch of earth

Where Europe's genius built a hearth;

The last and farthest flung outpost

'Gainst night and death and frost."

A boy, somewhat younger, followed this with a stirring recitation about a thick-headed peasant hero who, with a small troop, was placed to defend a bridge. All but five of this troop were killed and the order was given to return. The dull peasant leader did not understand and remained at his post alone until help came, when he died with a bullet in his heart.

Then came the most effective part of the program. A girl, a pupil in one of the higher grades, appeared dressed in the traditional dress of a certain portion of Finland, consisting of a white loose blouse and short full embroidered skirt. There was also a bodice and a colored fringed apron. She carried a kantele, a stringed instrument whose music is of a monotonous and rather melancholy tone. This served as the accompaniment to two or three folk songs, which she half sang, half recited in a way that brought forth special applause. Coffee and cakes, carefully prepared by the members of the Cooking Classes, were then served, after which games were played and riddles given. Among the latter was Maja's favorite: "What can't speak yet tells the truth?" Answer. — Scales.

The next Guest Night was devoted entirely to the "Kalevala," that wonderful national epic made up of the folk songs gathered by Elias Lönnrot. It began with a tableau in which was seen Wäinämöinen, the ancient bard of the poem, "renowned for singing and magic"; Ilmarinen, the children's favorite hero, a wonderful smith; Kullervo, the wicked shepherd, whose hand was against every man's; the jolly, reckless Lemminkainen, and Louhi, the mistress of Pohjola (the North) and her beautiful, much sought after daughter, the Rainbow Maiden. This was followed by the reading of a passage describing Wäinämöinen's playing,

"All the birds that fly in mid-air

Fell like snow flakes from the heavens,

Flew to hear the minstrel's playing

Hear the harp of Wäinämöinen."

Then came the description of how the eagle, the swans, the tiny finches and the fish, and all within hearing, were affected by the magic harp music.

The curtain dropped and rolled up again to show the meeting of Wäinämöinen and his envious rival Youkahainen, who wishes to fight. The tableau changed before the audience into an act in which Wäinämöinen's magic singing causes his rival to sink helplessly into quicksand, and in which he refuses every ransom Youkahainen offers, until it comes to Youkahainen's beauteous sister.

One of the pupils now read the parts from the "Kalevala" describing the various tasks that the heroes were called on to perform: the forging of the magic sampo, a coin, corn, and salt mill which could grind out good fortune for whoever had it; the capturing of the elk of Hiisi; the bridling of the fire-breathing horse, and others.

Last the teacher himself took the platform to call the attention of the audience to the beautiful expressions of mother love scattered throughout. He showed how even the wise Wäinämöinen thought first of his mother when in distress:

"If my mother were now breathing

She would surely truly tell me

How I might best bear this trouble,"

and how the mother love of the hot-headed Lemminkainen rescues him from death.

It was not always easy for Juhani and Maja to get to school, yet it was rarely that they or any of the other pupils were absent. Often the only light they had going and coming was that thrown up by the snow. Sometimes, however, the remarkable Northern Lights (the Aurora Borealis) helped the sun in its labors. They grew all the sturdier, too, for having to face wild weather.

All the pupils came to school on skis, made of long narrow pieces of wood with a leather strip in the center through which one merely slipped the foot, so that in falling the foot was released. The front end was pointed and curved upward. It does not take long to go a good distance on skis. Juhani could go seven miles an hour on his. There were always rows of skis at the school door, some large, some small, for the proper length depends on the height of the individual. To find it one stands with arms extended above one's head. The skis must reach from the ground to the raised fingertips.

At home one of the older children's duties was to teach a young brother or sister how to use skis. It was not unusual to see even three-year old babes on them. At five years most of them could be trusted alone. The first lesson was one of balance. One foot was placed in advance, the knees bent with the body forward. This was followed by making the first step.

Sometimes, during vacation days, there were ski races, but these were forgotten when in the latter part of November announcement was made of a ski jumping contest to be held in the nearest village. The age limit kept the smaller boys from all hope of taking part, but they at once organized a ski jumping contest of their own. Juhani was the youngest admitted even here. "No, I've never tried jumping," he confessed when asked, "but I know that I can do it." At the first meeting of the schoolboys he had an opportunity to show what he could do. He advanced with something like a swagger, made a good jump but landed in a heap instead of on his feet. His companions, who knew that there was something to learn, all shouted, "The cow cannot climb a hill! The cow cannot climb a hill!" which is an old proverb, and means that one cannot perform a feat beyond his ability.

Juhani picked himself up, shut his lips tightly together, and tried again and again until he could outdistance many of the boys.

When the day of the great contest came everybody who could went to see the sport. A strong little platform had been built on the side of a hill near the town. From this the contestants were to spring.

There were six competitors. One especially seemed to have won favor beforehand, not because he was better looking than the others, for he was not, but probably because of the merry good humor in his eyes.

The signal came to start. First came a stalwart, serious-faced youth who jumped over sixty feet, landed on his feet, and raced down the hill. After him followed three others, all of whom jumped between sixty-five and seventy-five feet. The fifth rushed after them, jumping seventy-nine feet, but failing to land on his feet. Last came the popular youth. He glanced around until he met the gaze of a little old lady in the crowd. Then he smiled and waved his hat to her, ran up on the platform, doubled up his legs, which he kept close together, and then waving his arms to keep his balance, jumped far forward. A shout of applause burst forth as he landed on his feet and raced down the hill. This increased stillmore when it was learned that he had out-distanced all the others, his jump being over eighty feet.

The last day of the term at school the children had a big Christmas tree. It was decorated with Russian and Finnish flags and candles and with sweets for all hanging from its branches. There were many visitors, for on this day prizes were to be awarded to the most deserving pupils. No one knew for certain to whom the chief prizes were to go, but there were often clever guesses. In Juhani's Grade, however, a murmur of surprise was heard when the name of the winner was announced. An unusually shy youth stepped forward awkwardly. Juhani remembered him as a poor boy who had entered that term. He remembered also how hard at first he had found the studies, then how he improved by degrees until he ranked with the best.

The teacher, in making the presentation, dwelt on the virtue of such perseverance andthen invited the visitors to ask him any questions in his late studies that they desired.

Several were eager to do this, much to the lad's embarrassment. But no sooner did he begin to answer than the embarrassment vanished, and he surprised all present by the clearness of his replies.

At the conclusion the teacher said: "This year we have for good reasons departed from our usual custom of presenting some book to be treasured by the winner. Instead we present to this deserving pupil a certain amount of money with only one stipulation, that he spend it in things that will most help him in his future studies."

"What will most help me in my future studies," the pupil responded, after some words of thanks, "will be the thought that my mother is more comfortable. So I accept this gladly if you have no objection to my giving it all at once to her."

The applause of all present showed their consent, and after an enquiring look at his teacher he walked up to a poorly-dressed woman who sat at the very rear of the room and whose eyes filled with tears as she took the money from his hands.

The younger children were not the only ones provided with schooling. In the nearest village to Juhani's home an adult school had been recently established by a big association called the Society for Popular Education. One half of the time each day was devoted to hand work, one half to easy conversational lessons in history, literature, science or any other study that appealed to the particular group gathered together. All social classes were represented in this school. There were sons of peasants, servants, shop-keepers. Some of the teachers were paid; others volunteered their services to help make life more pleasant and useful for their fellowmen. Among the latter was a rich neighbor who had just finished a course in one of the big Agriculture Schools of the country and was looking forward to having a farm of her own. Another teacher was plainly a university student, for she wore the regulation student cap, on which a golden lyre was embroidered. Much of the social life of this community centered about this school. The people came not only to study and learn but also to enjoy as a relief from hard daily work the companionship of others.

CHAPTER VI

THE DECEMBER VACATION

LONG before the coldest weather came, everything was made ready for a six or eight months' winter. The double windows were surrounded by cotton wool and gummed paper to keep out the draughts. The open rafters of the kitchen now served as a store room. From them hung dried fish, smoked pork, and even several weeks' supply of rye bread in large hard cakes with a hole in the middle of each.

As soon as the December holidays came, parties at neighboring houses followed each other in quick succession. Sometimes these were ski-ing parties of school children with the teacher in charge. Sometimes the older folks gathered, and sometimes whole families. There was always a dinner, and almost always dancing and the playing of games.

One day Juhani's whole family went to the home of a friend who lived fully ten miles distant. It was only about nine in the morning when they started in two low sleighs. The air was crisp and so still that it did not seem to stir, the sky intensely blue, as they hurried over snow-covered roads, past many forests, each tree bright in its pearly gown; past two farms whose buildings looked strikingly red and bare against their white background.

As they neared their destination, a bright-looking boy, accompanied by a kind of wolf hound, raced up on his skis to meet them. "You're just in time," he shouted when sufficiently near, "to help me make a fox trap. An old scamp of a fox has been after our chickens and I mean to get him."

"Where are you going to set the trap?" called back Juhani eagerly.

"I'm going to show you," responded the other, and as Juhani dismounted from the sleigh, the two made their way to some distance back of the barn. Here Juhani's friend had everything ready. First he drove a long stake into the ground. This stake was forked at the end with the central prong the longest. "Feel the edges," he said to Juhani.

Juhani did so and almost cut his finger. The edges were as sharp as knives.

"I don't understand yet," he said, putting his hand up to his mouth, "how that can catch a fox."

"Wait," returned his friend, and running to the barn he soon returned with bait which he placed at the top.

"The old fellow will jump at that," he explained, "and catch his paw between the prongs. You bet it'll hold him fast, too. There are a lot of them around," he continued as they made their way to the house, "and we're a good deal put out by them. Grandfather says, however, that it is nothing to the time when father first moved here. Then there were wolves and bears. I'd like to meet a bear. Do you remember the lines:

'Otso apple of the forest

With thy honey paws so curving'?

Grandfather says that they used to use charms to help them when they went hunting. Do you know what he likes to talk about better than bear hunting? It's seal shooting; perhaps because he did it only once. It wasn't here, of course, but on the frozen sea. He says he lay flat on a sled in front of which he had fastened a white sail so that the seal would take it for a part of the ice around. He pushed the sled with his feet, and, when near enough, shot."

"That was when he was a fisherman," conjectured Juhani.

His friend laughed. "Please don't use the past tense in regard to him. Why, he's still a fisherman. Only last year he had a fishing adventure that would make some people's hair rise. You look as if you didn't believe. Come, I'll get him to tell you about it."

They found the old man sitting in a sunny workroom mending a basket. He was quite ready to talk. "I don't belong here," he said, "but to the east end of the gulf. You say that you want to hear what happened last spring. Well, a whole camp of us went out together to fish through the ice. That's done every year. We took tents and firewood and food and expected to stay a long time. It was all right for a while and we got a lot of fish. But the spring thaw came earlier than we expected; we had fellows watching, but they were careless, and the first thing we knew the ice had cracked and I and one other were carried out to sea on a great ice floe. Our companions saw us when we were about twelve yards away, but they couldn't do anything for they hadn't any boats. We couldn't do anything but let the wind and wave carry us wherever they wished. I had a bottle of rum in my pocket and a big hunk of hard bread. My companion had nothing but a plug of tobacco. These three things we divided and lived on for two days. At last we drifted to firm ice, from which, stiff as we were, we managed to make our way to the mainland."

"You don't expect to go this year, do you?" asked Juhani.

"Yes, I do. Right after the holidays. Why shouldn't I?" asked the old man sharply. "I wasn't drowned, was I?"

Right here they were fortunately called into the house. When they reached it, Juhani at once noticed that it was some one's name day, for the doors were prettily decorated with boughs. A big meal awaited them indoors, and here Juhani found that the decorations were in honor of the mother for her chair was also wreathed. He at once went up to her and offered his congratulations, which the other members of his family had had a chance to do before.

A long time was spent at the table. When the meal was finished each person went up to the host and hostess, shook hands with them and said "Tack," thank you.

Juhani's friend next took him for a visit to the farm's carpenter shop, where he showed him the posts and gates he was making. "Are you going to have the shoemaker come to your place this year?" he asked. "We expect him here next week to make us enough shoes to last the year through. The tailor isn't coming till January. Two weeks ago we had the harness maker; I had to help him, and I tell you, I'm glad the harness is mended."

Here he thought of something else with which to entertain his guest. "Why, you haven't seen my new toboggan slide. Let's go quick."

They stopped at the barn to get a sled and then had several merry rides down a short but steep hill. This was followed by snow-balling and fancy ski jumping until time to bid each other good-by.

A few days following this pleasant visit, Juhani, Maja and the older sister attended a "Riddle Evening" at the home of a much nearer neighbor. Here quite a number of young people were gathered, each trying to be called the Master Riddle Guesser. Whoever couldn't answer three riddles in succession had to play the fool. He was seated in a chair in the middle of the room. One of the girls handed over her embroidered apron and it was tied around his waist. Another took off the kerchief around her neck and it was put on his head. Still another lent her glass beads. A saucer was then held over a candle flame until soot collected and with this his face was painted. The jolly company circled around him jeering and then forming a procession solemnly escorted him from the room and bade him study out the answers that he had not been able to guess.

CHAPTER VII

CHRISTMAS WEEK

SEVERAL days before Christmas, the whole farmhouse was scrubbed and cleaned, while bread was baked and ale brewed.

On Christmas Eve little Maja scattered clean straw on all the floors.

"Don't forget the birds," her older sister cautioned her.

"As if I would!" responded Maja. Nodding to Juhani, who stood by the door, she carried out a basket filled with crumbs and grain for the wild birds and animals. Juhani soon followed her with a sheaf of corn, which he placed where it would be sure to attract.

"You haven't forgotten, have you, Juhani," said Maja somewhat breathlessly as they stood together, "that they all can speak to-night?"

Juhani nodded and was silent for a moment. It always took him some time to get stirred up enough to talk. Then he said slowly, "I've put some of the food near the door, for 'tis said that if you listen behind it at night you'll be able to understand what they say. Don't tell, but I'm going to listen. Wouldn't it be hunky if I found out some secret?"

"Oh, then I must listen, too!" exclaimed Maja. But her brother did not like the idea.

"We'd be found out sure if you did," he said. "Better let me do it alone and I'll tell you about it to-morrow,—before I tell any one else."

Maja reluctantly agreed, and the two went indoors where they separated, each to wrap up presents that they had made and to write the name of the recipient together with an appropriate verse or sentence on an attached paper. These were placed in the front room from which they mysteriously disappeared while the family were having their supper of rice porridge and lut fisk (stock fish), prepared in a way peculiar to the country.

After supper all seated themselves near the big stove and were very still with their eyes on the door. Presently a loud knock came. "Welcome! Welcome!" every one shouted.

The door opened and Father Christmas dressed as a Yule Goat entered. He carried a basket filled with gifts, and as he took one after another up he first read the recipient's name, then the attached verse, some of which were so funny that they caused much laughter. No one was left out. The servants, who were all present, smiled happily at having been remembered so generously, and even the big dog came in for his share which was a piece of meat wrapped securely in paper.

When bed time came, the children prepared to go to sleep on straw in memory of the Christ Child. Maja looked regretfully after Juhani, who had received permission from his mother to have the straw for him placed that night on the kitchen floor.

In the morning all rose early, Maja and Juhani running into the front room to see "Heaven," a framework hung from the ceiling and made up of threads and yarn and straws and decorated with gilt stars. It was lit by a candle and seemed very beautiful to both of them, much to the satisfaction of the older sister, who had followed them, and whose work it was.

Long before six o'clock a visit had been paid to all the farm animals, and a supply of food and some dainty given each. Candles were then placed in all the windows, and putting on their heavy coats, their caps with ear flappers, and their heavy boots, they all piled into sleighs and were off to church.

It was very dark much of the way. Indeed it would be fortunate if the sun shone for five or six hours before night. They did not mind the dark, for they were not alone. From all sides people came, either on skis or in sleighs.

After the service there was a race of skis and sleighs homewards over the frozen lake in eager anticipation of the Christmas dinner, whose chief dish, Maja whispered to Juhani, was to be a big ham. It was not until they were home again that she found a chance to corner Juhani by himself and demand eagerly: "What did they say?"

Juhani looked curiously at her. "I listened last night," he said slowly, "for a long time but I didn't hear any animal or bird speak." Then, seeing Maja's disappointed face, he added quickly, "There are other things one can do. You know Esko's grandmother. Well, she once saw a great assembly of snakes on a hill near Impivaare. She knows all about snakes. She says that if you can kill an old adder and eat him just before the first cuckoo, ever after that you'll understand the language of birds and know all sorts of things."

Maja shuddered. "You wouldn't do that, would you?" she asked appealingly.

Juhani looked at her for a moment, and then, unable to withstand the temptation to tease her, said, "Why not?" and ran away.

Before New Year's with its special significance came, a guest arrived from Helsingfors. It was Juhani and Maja's aunt, a woman who had achieved some renown in the Capital as an architect.

They enjoyed her vivid descriptions of how the snow there was daily shoveled from the pavements, and how when you step on what remains it screams: "A hard winter! A hard winter!"

"We haven't gone in for as much ice yachting as usual," she remarked, rather sadly, the children thought. "The times are too unsettled."

"Tell us about the yachting," urged Maja, seeing the look of interest in Juhani's face, and knowing his slowness in asking for what he wanted.

"I know nothing more thrilling," the aunt returned, smiling, "than lying flat on your stomach on an ice yacht in motion. The yacht may take little leaps so that at times it seems to you as if it were about to fly. Then you rush madly at something and prepare yourself surely for a smash, but just in time the yacht swerves and you are safe to fly some more. In a sense you do fly, for when the wind is strong the yacht is sometimes lifted high into the air. When it comes down you feel as if the world were coming to an end. It would have been fine for ice yachting this year, for we had black ice."

"What is that?" asked Maja.

"I know," broke in Juhani unexpectedly. "It is when the ice forms before snow falls."

His aunt nodded. "Yes; then the water looks like a mirror and it is much smoother than when covered with snow."

"Did you come direct from Helsingfors?" asked Lilja after a pause.

"No," replied the aunt. "I had to go first to Viborg." And she described to them the famous Saima Canal, one of the many canals of the country which starts from there. It is built of Finnish granite and took eleven years to complete. "It goes," she said, "to Saima Lake, called the lake of a thousand islands, the most important lake of Finland. This lake is about three hundred feet above the sea level, so that the vessels on the canal have to be raised by locks. There are at least twenty-eight of these. I once saw three steamers on it and they looked as if they were walking up stairs. We mustn't forget that this canal is one of the good things that we owe to the Russians. It probably would not have been constructed but for the interest of Tzar Nicolas I, during whose reign it was begun. Viborg seems to be made up of Russian soldiers, which of course is no wonder, since it is the nearest town to the Russian frontier."

She seemed inclined to say more but evidently thought better of it for she changed the conversation. "Some friends with whom I had dinner at Viborg told me a story that will interest you. It was regarding a relative that they called Pekka (Peter) and who for a while lived in the Castle of Olafsborg in the quaint town of Nyslott. It happened in this way. He came to Nyslott to attend the Musical Festival held there in the summer. The town was crowded and he despaired of getting a bed when he ran across an acquaintance to whom he told his troubles.

"'Unfortunately,' said the latter, 'I am a stranger here. I don't know a person, — except the watchman who has charge of the Castle.'

"The relative is of a somewhat romantic turn of mind. 'Excellent!' he said. 'Just the thing. Let's go over at once and hire a room from the watchman.'

"'Do you mean,' said his acquaintance incredulously, 'that you're willing to stay in a ruined castle — probably haunted — all night?'

"But the young man was stubborn, and the two secured a boat and rowed over to the Castle. Nyslott is built on islands but the castle has one of its own. When they landed they found the watchman, who, after some hesitation, offered the stranger his own room, which was in a separate little building put up for his benefit.

"But Pekka would not have it so. 'I'd rather you'd fix me up something in the castle itself.' The watchman thought this a joke and proposed that they wander through the building to find a place that would suit.

"So they started. Everything looked very ancient, for the castle dates back to 1475. They went through queer passages where the walls were sometimes fifteen feet thick, under arches, up winding stairs, down again, into cellars and dungeons and ruined chambers. At last they came to the Hall of Knights, a long, dimly lighted room. The walls had fallen here to enclose partly a little space that was still roofed over.

"'This shall be my lodging place,' declared the young man. 'Are you serious?' asked the watchman.

"'I certainly am,' answered Pekka, putting some money in the watchman's hand. The watchman thought for a while. 'I shall have to see the authorities,' he said at last.

"'I'll wait here,' said Pekka, and wait he did.

"When the guardian of the place returned he was all smiles. 'All right,' he said and set to work clearing the space. Then he brought rugs and a big fur coat on which the man could sleep.

"The weather was warm and the bed couldn't have been very uncomfortable, for Pekka stayed there three nights. He declared afterwards that he dreamt wonderful dreams of the time when three races, the Swedes, the Russians and the Finns, struggled for the possession of this spot. One night he awoke shouting: 'The enemy! the enemy!' and then found that the invaders were only some of the many bats, who thought that they had a better right than he to this castle home."

Here the aunt brought forth some interesting photographs which she had taken at Helsingfors. One was an active scene at the open air market when the autumn sailing fleet came to sell winter provisions. It showed the peasant carts and the bright stalls covered with white awnings and blue umbrellas, the market women in gay attire, the butchers in bright pink coats or blouses, and the boats laden with fruit and vegetables, kegs of salted fish, and honey. There was also a picture taken earlier in the year, showing one of the principal harbors with crafts of every shape and size. There were enormous passenger boats, little market boats rowed by bare-armed women, small pleasure yachts, big timber ships with red brown sails, and a group of white Russian war vessels.

She had pictures, too, in which the older members of the family were interested, showing two very distinct styles of architecture to be found in Helsingfors. One was of a group of fine modern buildings on a broad street called the Myntgatan. They were of gray stone, six or seven stories high, dignified and well proportioned, with carefully selected classical decorations. In contrast to this, she produced photographs of other buildings of decided Finnish individuality. These buildings showed great variety, being of rough granite or brick, with tiled roofs, unusual balconies and porticos, fantastic plaster decorations, such as a group of frogs, a procession of swimming swans, a bunch of carrots and turnips, or a savage animal head.

Another group of pictures showed the types of work done by Helsingfors women. In one of these a number of women were cleaning the streets, using immense brooms for the sweeping. In one, they were washing clothes on platforms built out into the sea. In still another, several stood on a scaffold, plastering a house, while three others were at work constructing a door.

Of all the pictures Maja liked best a view of the statue of Runeberg, the national poet, showing how it was decorated with flowers and laurels on the anniversary of his birthday. Juhani was attracted more particularly to a picture of a magnificent horse harnessed to a sleigh, his loins covered with a cloak coming far down to keep out the cold.

The aunt presented these to the children. "Our people are kind to their horses," she said to Juhani; then turning to Maja: "On Runeberg's birthday not only is his statue in the square decorated, but all houses are lit up to show he is remembered, while in every restaurant people give festal dinners in his honor."

Then the aunt brought forth something that the children appreciated still more than the pictures. It was a sort of cake, especially peculiar to Viborg, made in the form of a lover's knot, and it had been baked on straw, some of which still stuck to the bottom.

CHAPTER VIII

SUMMER TIME

IN April the melting snow and ice showed that spring was on the way. How dirty and muddy it was everywhere! Instead of skis, the children had to wade to school in well greased boots.

New kinds of festivities took the place of the old. At Easter time eggs were painted and the family feasted on memma, a dish of boiled sweetened malt, eaten with cream and sugar.

On the first of May big swings were erected in the grove near the church and there the people gathered from a considerable distance, the children to swing and frolic, and their elders to listen to the singing of runes, some so ancient that the meaning was no longer plain, or to speeches welcoming the return of spring.

"Let's play! Let's play!" the children shouted as if they hadn't also played in the winter. Play they did. Sometimes it was "Last Pair Out." In this the boys and girls formed pairs and stood behind each other. At a signal the last couples separated, each going on different sides of the line and trying to unite in front before being caught by the one who was "It." They danced "To-day is the First of May" in a double circle, and the "Ring Dance" to which they sang:

My love is like a strawberry,

So red and sweet is she:

And no one else may swing her round,

No one else 'cept me.

There was one little girl who was quite a leader in the games. Perhaps the reason was the enthusiastic way in which she played. She seemed to have two favorites: "Hide and Seek," in which the children counted out to see who was to be "It," and "Wolf." Both boys and girls played the latter as they did most of the other games. Juhani was the first to be the "Wolf," to the apparent joy of the leader, who took particular delight in teasing and escaping from him until he just ran her down and caught her.

Maja did not play this. She had found some children younger than herself whom she joined in making miniature farms out of stones and sand. The first building which she erected was not the dwelling-house but the Sauna or bath-house. Then followed the other farm buildings, and last the cattle had stones carefully selected for them.

The spring, ushered in with such hearty welcome, went with a surprising swiftness, and summer arrived with intense blue skies and floods of sunshine and flowers. This was the time of the white nights,—a happy holiday time,—when the sun shines for more than eighteen hours at a time and for the remainder of the twenty-four leaves generously its reflection behind.

During this springtime weather Maja saw that there were fresh wild flowers—pansies, lilies of the valley, lilacs, or wild roses—daily in the living-room. She loved the spring particularly for these. "How I love the flowers!" she would exclaim enthusiastically to Juhani whenever she found a new one.

Juhani would smile slowly, look thoughtfully into the distance, and after a pause return: "I like the spring for many things, but best I think for the change in the forest." Maja knew that he meant the new bits of sunshine everywhere and the new growth of needles that glistened so green against the background of the dark pines, and all the new bird calls to be heard there.

In June the schools closed, and for a while nothing was talked of but the preparations for the great midsummer festival to be held on June twenty-fourth, John the Baptist Day.

There seemed no end of things to be done to show gladness. Maja wove garlands of flowers, while Juhani and his friends cut down great branches of birch trees in the forest, with which to decorate the houses. Lilja and her girl friends were also busy. They went to the fields and wound colored yarn around the rye stalks, arranging them to indicate joy and sorrow, love and hate. Before the grain was harvested these marked stalks would be found and the year's fortune foretold according to which was highest.

Big bonfires, called kokko, were lit on all the highest points, and also on rafts on the lake in honor of the Sun. These were kept burning for twenty-four hours, for it is considered unlucky for them to go out sooner. Around these the people gathered to dance, many of them coming from a distance in farm carts trimmed with birch and filled with hay. There was a feast, too, of warm soup, cold salmon, and fancy cakes. The swings must not be forgotten. Several of them had been erected and not merely for the children. On some, young men and women swung together, while they sang the beautiful melancholy songs about this beautiful fleeting time.

During this season tourists invaded the country districts, some on their way to Aavasaksa Hill where the sun can then be seen at midnight, shedding gray, faintly luminous rays. Among those who came were many Russians of the wealthy and middle classes.

It was not all play. There was much, very much hard work in which the children all had their set tasks. Juhani had to drive the cattle through the woodlands, assist Lilja with the milking, and help make hay. Maja had to gather berries, of which there was a great abundance. It is true there were compensations for all these tasks. If children had to gather berries, they could also eat big bowls of them with thick cream added, at every meal. Some of the berries Maja gathered she sold to passengers on the lake steamers. When she intended doing so, she made birch baskets for them by stripping off a foot square of bark and bending it into the shape of a box without a lid, then sewing the sides with twigs.

She had also to gather sacks full of luikku, a soft white cotton flower with an odd perfume, to be used for stuffing the family pillows.

Although it was vacation there was one school task that all the children had to do or cared to do. It was gathering, pressing, and mounting as many as possible of the numerous wild flowers everywhere found in the woods and fields. The best presented at the beginning of the school term were always put on exhibition.

The only disagreeable part of the warm weather was the annoyance from mosquitoes. This made it necessary to light smoldering fires for the protection of the cattle who seemed to appreciate the fires, for without being driven they would cluster around them. Twigs of juniper were burned in the house for the same purpose. It was not always easy to get juniper, for it grows only in clay soil and Maja and her friends sometimes had a long tramp after it.

Once, remembering the story of the Lapp children, Juhani smeared tar all over his face and hands and then teased Maja by threatening to put some on her too.

After July, the long magic days grew shorter, and when the days and nights were again almost equal, the children found themselves planning what they would do when school reopened.

THE END